Pioneers in Cell Biology

Elizabeth R. C. Cregan

Life Science Readers: Pioneers in Cell Biology

Publishing Credits

Editorial Director
Dona Herweck Rice

Associate Editor
Joshua BishopRoby

Editor-in-Chief
Sharon Coan, M.S.Ed.

Creative Director
Lee Aucoin

Illustration Manager
Timothy J. Bradley

Publisher
Rachelle Cracchiolo, M.S.Ed.

Science Contributor
Sally Ride Science™

Science Consultants
Thomas R. Ciccone, B.S., M.A.Ed.,
Chino Hills High School
Dr. Ronald Edwards,
DePaul University

Teacher Created Materials
5301 Oceanus Drive
Huntington Beach, CA 92649-1030
http://www.tcmpub.com

ISBN 978-0-7439-0586-2

Printed in Malaysia
Thumbprints.42806

Table of Contents

Anton van Leeuwenhoek

(1632–1723)

Anton van Leeuwenhoek

Nothing about Anton van Leeuwenhoek's (AN-tahn vahn LAY-vuhn-hook) early life would suggest the amazing contribution he made to the science of cell biology. He was born in Holland. His father was a basket maker. His mother's family worked as brewers. He went to school when young, but he did not attend college. At 16, he started to work with a linen draper. By the age of 22, he returned to his hometown, where he stayed the rest of his life.

Leeuwenhoek started his own business as a draper. He sold fabric. He also had many odd jobs. He worked as a surveyor and city official. He even took care of a friend's estate after the man died.

Leeuwenhoek's microscopes look very different from microscopes today!

Leeuwenhoek holding one of his microscopes

Leeuwenhoek spoke Dutch. He never learned other languages. The cards were stacked against him. There was no reason that he should have been able to make it in the scientific community. He lacked the money and education. He didn't speak other languages. But he had skill, and he worked hard. He was very curious, too.

One thing in his favor is that he learned a valuable trade. He learned to grind lenses. This skill came in handy. He used it to make simple microscopes. He started to observe things with them. He got interested in microscopes after seeing a book by Robert Hooke. Hooke had invented a simple microscope. His book included pictures that fascinated Leeuwenhoek.

Take a Closer Look

Nine of Leeuwenhoek's microscopes exist today. They can magnify things to 270 times their size.

Dust Mites

Dust mites live on all of us. You can't see them without a microscope, though. They are on our skin. They are in our noses. They are even on our pets. They live in our carpets and our sheets!

Leeuwenhoek created one of the best microscopes available in the 17th century. He used his microscope to study living organisms. He made more than 400 microscopes. His were made of silver and copper frames. Some of his microscopes could magnify things to 270 times their size! Other microscopes of his day did much less. They could only magnify things about 20 to 30 times.

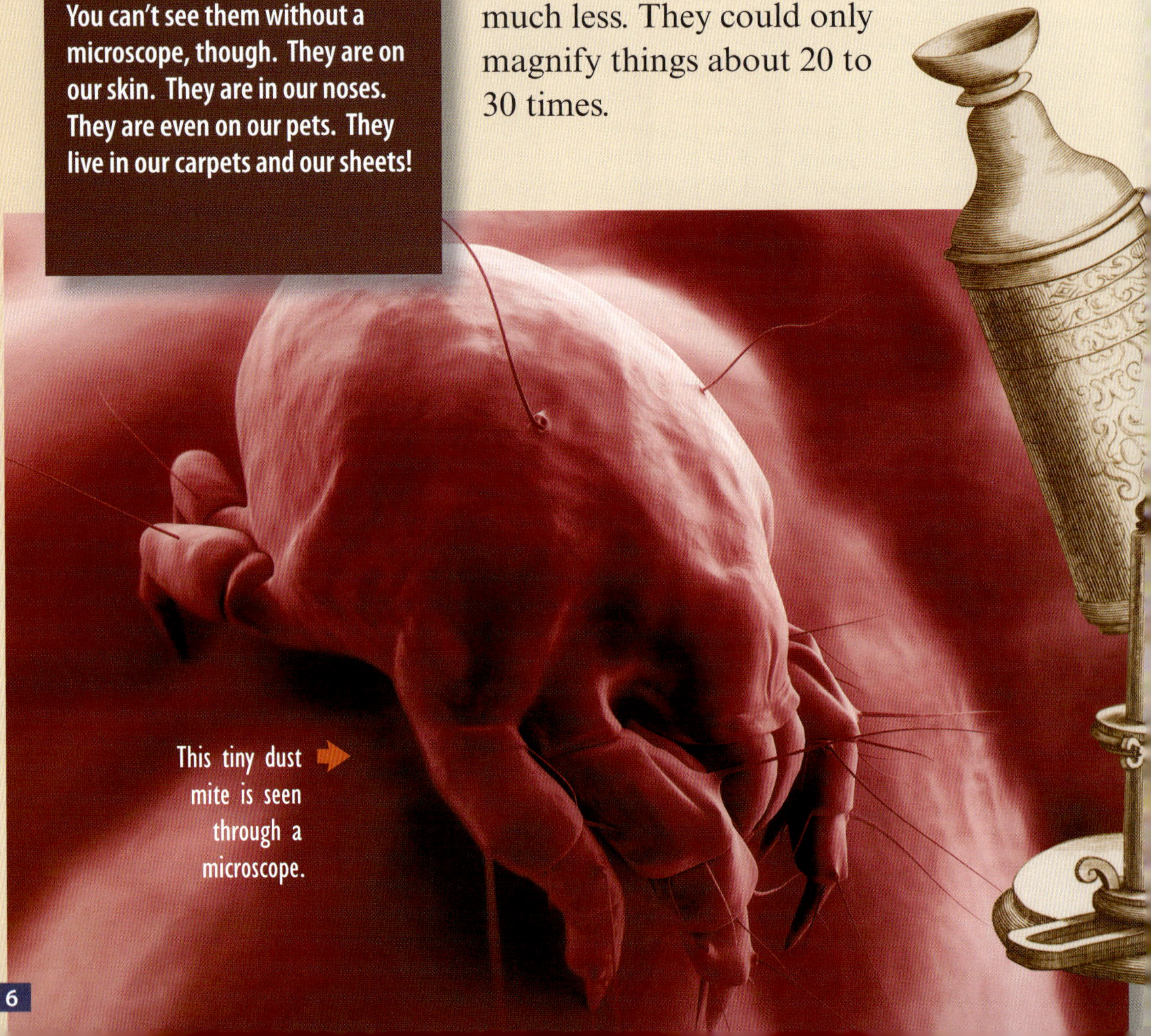

This tiny dust mite is seen through a microscope.

Robert Hooke (1635–1703)

Robert Hooke was born in England. At the age of 30, he invented a simple microscope called the compound-light microscope. It had three lenses. It could magnify things to 30 times their size. He also built the first telescope.

Hooke examined many things. One of the things he looked at was a piece of cork. Cork is made of dead wood. Through a microscope, it looks like rows of tiny boxes. These boxes reminded Hooke of something. He thought they looked like the tiny rooms that monks lived in at their **monasteries**. The rooms were called **cellula**. That's where we get the word ***cell***.

Hooke was the first scientist to observe cells and give them their name. But he did not understand how important cells were to the study of living things.

Hooke's simple microscope

Monks lived in small rooms such as this, called cellula.

These are some of the strange creatures that Leeuwenhoek discovered.

Leeuwenhoek paid great attention to the things he saw. He wasn't a good artist. So, he hired someone to draw pictures of what he saw. He would describe things like muscle fibers. He had the artist draw blood flowing in tiny veins. The veins were called **capillaries**. He also had the artist draw one-celled organisms gliding about in pond water. He named them **animalcules**.

Leeuwenhoek's work was amazing for his time. He was among the first to study single cells. But it would take two hundred more years before other scientists understood how important cells were to the study of organisms.

motor neuron

Naming the Nucleus

Robert Brown studied the cells of orchids. He saw small spots in the orchid cells. Then he looked at the cells of other plants. He saw the same spots. He called them *nuclei*. The singular word, **nucleus**, comes from the Latin word meaning "little nut."

Long Cells

Motor neurons are the longest cells in humans. They can be up to four and a half feet long! They start at the lower spinal cord. They end at the big toe.

Leeuwenhoek studied many things. He looked at lake water. He found more microorganisms there. He looked at animal and plant tissue. He observed mineral crystals. And he examined fossils. He found many interesting things.

Can you imagine where one of his most interesting findings was? It was on teeth. He looked at the plaque on his own teeth. He said it was as thick as batter. He also looked at the plaque on two women, and he looked at the teeth of two old men. The men had never cleaned their teeth! He found lots of little things moving around. They were tiny animalcules. In the men, he found more than he could imagine. Do you know what he was seeing? He was among the first to record findings about living bacteria.

Leeuwenhoek described things in great detail. You can imagine them perfectly when you read his descriptions.

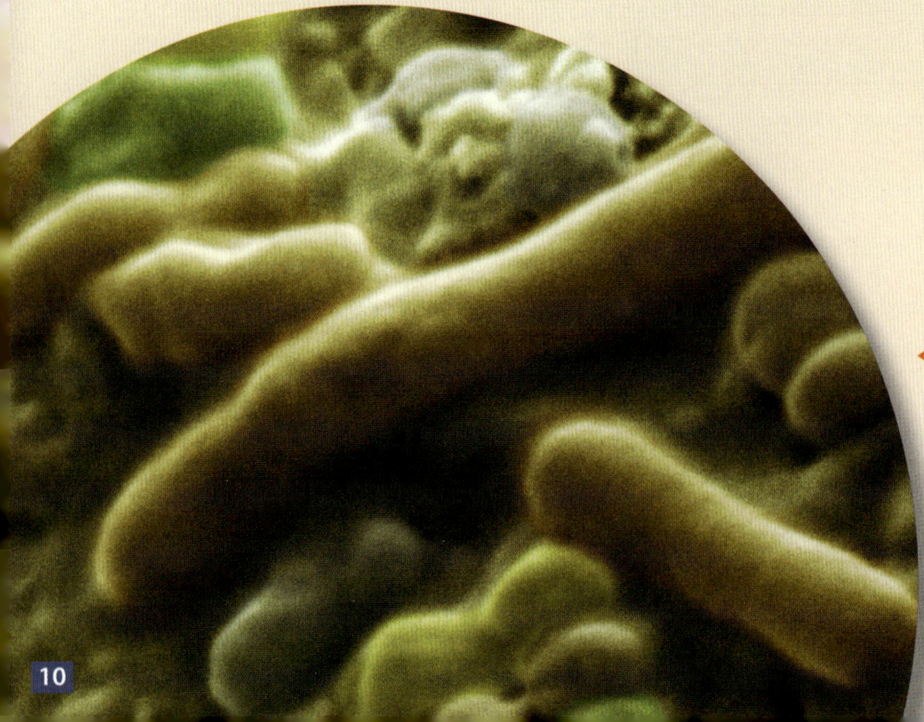

Bacterial tooth plaque is a very good reason to brush your teeth often!

Studying the Nucleus

Johann Friedrich Miescher (MY-shur) lived from 1844 to 1895. He was a doctor. He was also a chemist and biologist.

Miescher's father and uncle were important doctors. Miescher himself was partially deaf. He thought his hearing loss would be a disadvantage as a doctor. So, instead of practicing medicine, he studied the nuclei of cells.

Miescher decided to study white blood cells. These cells protect the body. They destroy germs as they enter the blood. Miescher needed many white blood cells in order to study their nuclei.

Pus is made of white blood cells. So, Miescher went to nearby hospitals to gather dirty bandages. The bandages were covered with pus. He washed the pus off the bandages. He then collected the white blood cells in beakers. He used chemicals to filter out the nuclei of the cells.

Miescher discovered a substance. He called it nuclein. Today we call this **DNA**. It is the chemical that helps organisms pass traits from one generation to the next. His work paved the way for future scientists to learn more about DNA.

Out of This World

Do you know how much DNA you have inside your cells? If you stretch it all out, it would reach to the moon 6,000 times!

August Weismann (1834–1914)

August Weismann (AW-goost VICE-mahn) was born in Germany. His father was a high school teacher. His mother was the daughter of the mayor. He began music lessons at the age of four. His piano teacher was a butterfly collector. The young Weismann became interested in this hobby. He wanted to study the natural sciences. But there were few jobs in the field. Someone suggested he study medicine. His mother had inherited money. She was able to pay for his medical studies.

Weismann became a medical officer in the military. He got married and had a son. Later, he was the personal doctor for a former duke. He was a lecturer and a professor. He was also the director of a zoological institute.

Butterfly collecting got Weismann into science.

Walther Flemming (1843–1905)

Walther Flemming was born in Germany. He was the only boy in his family. He had four sisters. His father was a psychiatrist. Flemming went to medical school. He then served in the military. He worked as a doctor there for one year. Later, he became a teacher at a university.

Flemming was a scientist. In 1879, he stained some cells. He looked at them under the microscope. The stain stuck to the nuclei of the cells. This made it very easy for him to study the nuclei.

He decided to stain cells that were growing. He looked at these cells under the light microscope. He could see them dividing. He saw the **chromosomes** come into view as stubby rods. Then, he saw them double in number. Next, half the chromosomes moved to each end of the cell. The chromosomes spread out like threads. He decided to name the process **mitosis**. Flemming was the first scientist to watch living cells divide.

Threads

Mitosis comes from the Greek word mitos, or thread. Chromosomes look like thread when cells divide.

sea urchin

Weismann studied sea urchins. They are multicellular organisms. He believed they are made of two kinds of cells. He thought they were made of germ cells and body cells. Germ cells pass along genetic information to offspring. Egg and sperm are germ cells. Body cells perform the work needed to keep the organism alive.

He realized that germ cells must join to create offspring. So each germ cell could only have half the number of chromosomes found in the body cells. He named this division of sex cells **reduction division**. It is now called **meiosis** (my-OH-sis).

Other people started looking at his work. This led them to return to the work of another scientist. They started to look at Gregor Mendel's work. He was a pioneer in the study of **genetics**.

This illustration from the late 1800s shows the characteristics with which Mendel worked.

Gregor Mendel

Gregor Mendel (MEN-duhl) was an Austrian monk who loved nature. He lived from 1822 to 1884. Mendel grew nearly 28,000 pea plants. He tested them to learn how plants pass traits to their offspring. He found that each new pea plant had different combinations of traits. His findings led to the study of genetics. Scientists did not realize how important Mendel's ideas were until the 20th century.

Gene Troubles

There are many genetic disorders. There is even one that makes people smell like rotting fish!

Joan Wright Goodman

(1925–2006)

Joan Wright Goodman was born in El Paso, Texas. She lived there until the age of 16, when she went to college in New York. She earned her degree in chemistry and then her doctorate degree. While there, she met her husband, a **physicist**. Together they moved to Tennessee and had two children.

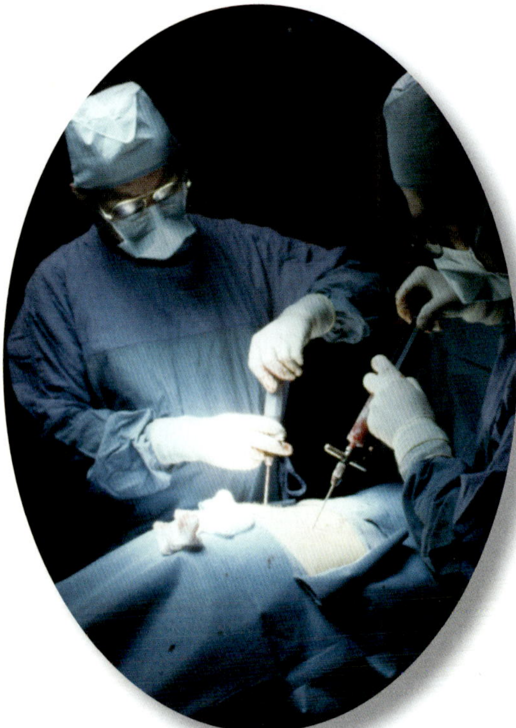

a bone marrow transplant

Goodman was the first to show that stem cells from bone marrow flow in the blood of mammals. This paved the way for current research on stem cells. A stem cell is a master cell. It can become any type of cell in the body.

Goodman studied bone marrow transplants. She researched their effects at fighting damage from **radiation**. She also studied immune response in cells.

Number of Chromosomes

Humans have 46 chromosomes. Fruit flies have eight. You might think this is because humans are more complex than fruit flies. But crayfish have 200 chromosomes. And giant sequoia trees have 22.

Thomas Hunt Morgan
(1866–1945)

In the 1900s, many scientists began to study chromosomes. They studied what happens during cell division. Thomas Hunt Morgan was an American scientist. He studied the chromosomes of fruit flies. Scientists like to use fruit flies in their experiments. Fruit flies have just eight chromosomes. They are easy to study under a light microscope. This makes the scientists' complicated work easier to manage.

Morgan developed the idea that chromosomes carry **genes**. The genes provide the blueprint to pass traits to offspring. He also identified special chromosomes. He named them X and Y.

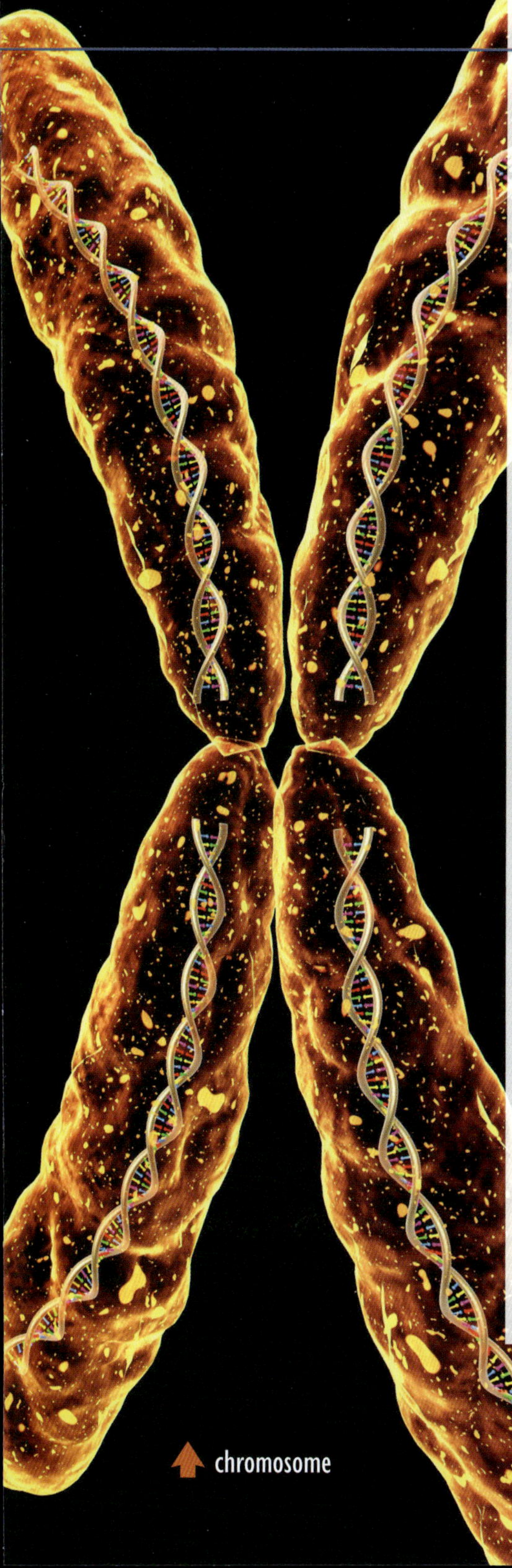

chromosome

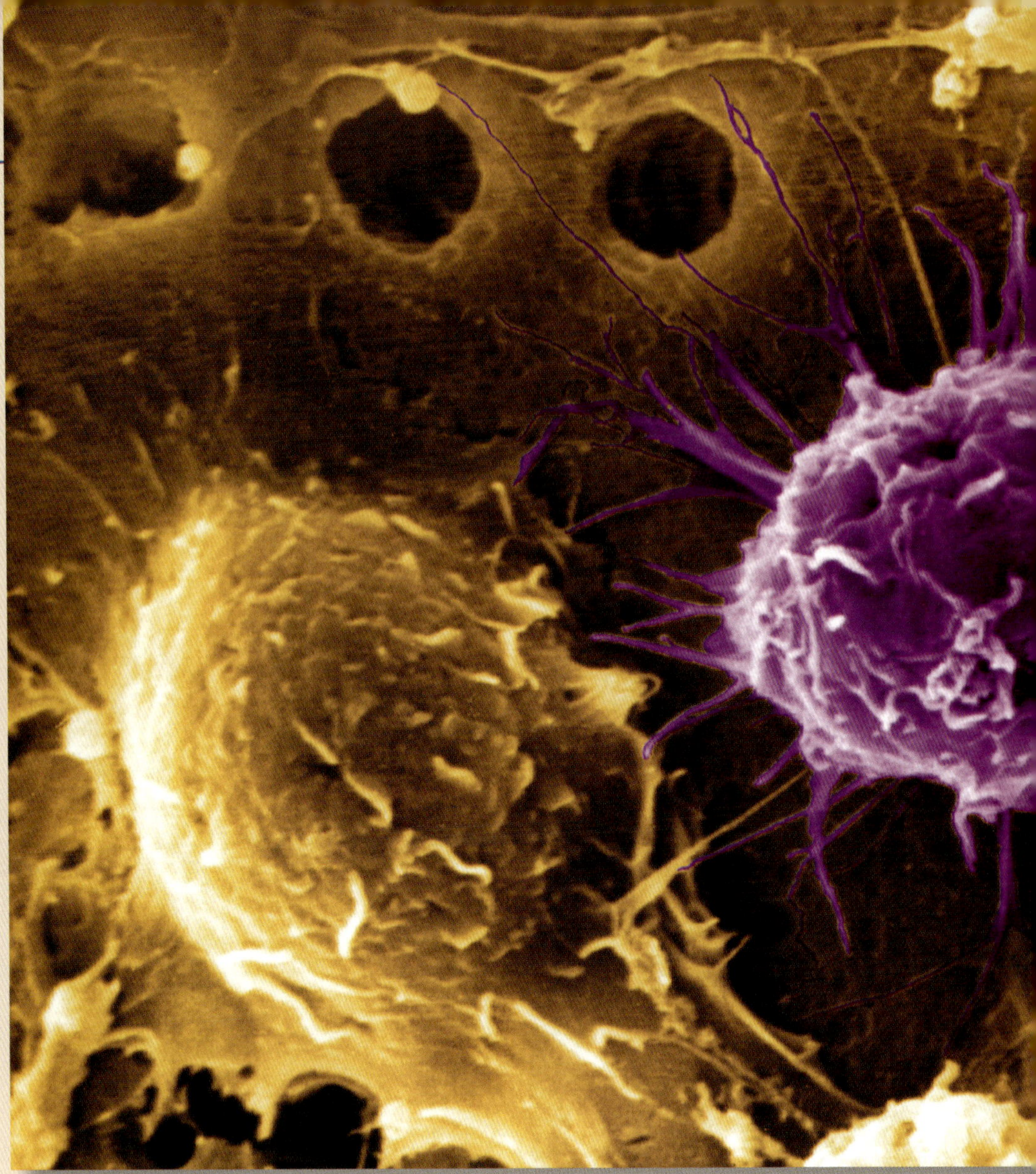

Goodman and her family later moved to California. She continued her research. She also became known as a strong supporter of women in science. It was important to her to support the work of others.

Goodman retired at the age of 61. But she was far from done. She was full of energy and enthusiasm. She entered law school, earned her law degree, and passed the bar exam. She

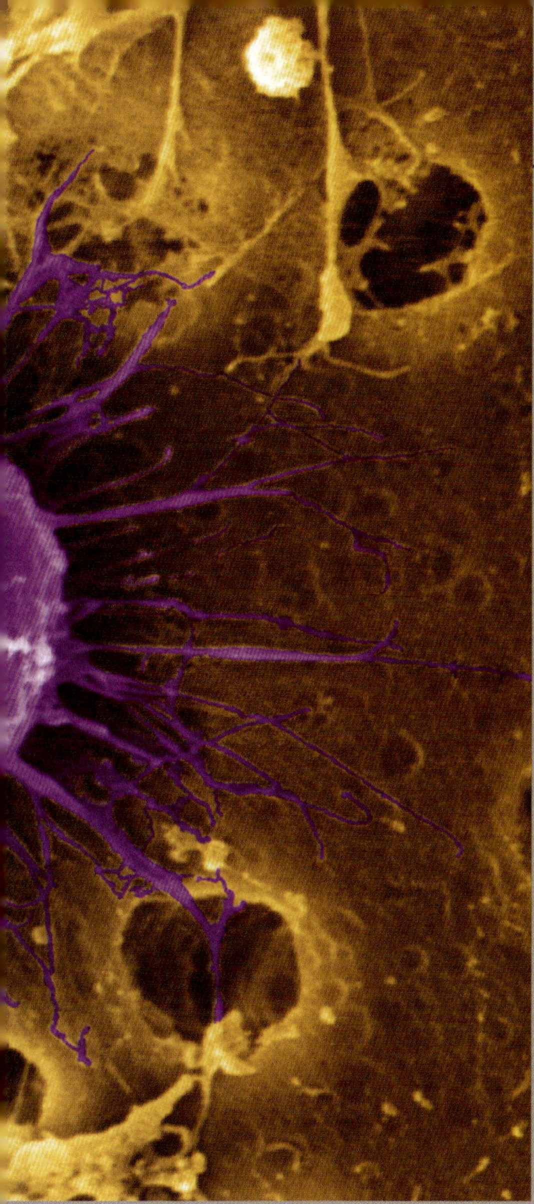

A stem cell from human bone marrow is shown in purple.

decided not to practice law, though. Instead, she and her husband became patrons of the arts.

Goodman died in 2006. She will always be remembered for her contributions to stem cell research and her support of science and the arts.

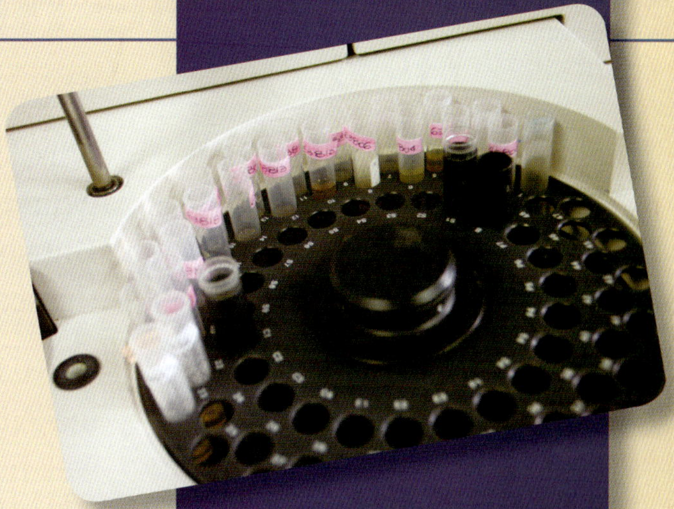

The Centrifuge

A centrifuge (SEN-truh-fyooj) spins around. It spins like a washing machine. It spins fast. Any liquid in the material is separated out. This centrifuge is able to spin at very high speeds. It separates large molecules. This makes it easier for scientists to study them.

Going for a Ride

There is a Mission: SPACE ride at Disney's EPCOT center in Florida. It uses a giant centrifuge. It's just for fun! Riders spin around at high speeds. They get to see what it feels like to travel into outer space.

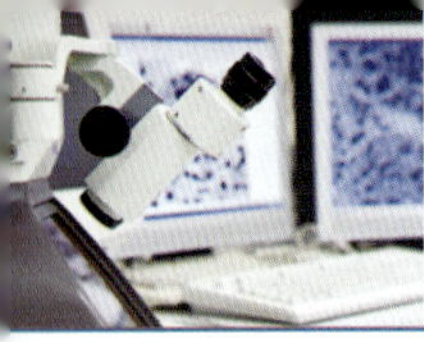

Christiane Nusslein-Volhard

(1942–)

Nusslein-Volhard also plays the flute.

You wouldn't know from Christiane Nusslein-Volhard's early life that she would end up earning a Nobel Prize. But she did. It was for research on genes that cause birth defects.

Christiane Nusslein-Volhard (kris-tee-AH-nuh NYS-lahn-FAWL-hart) was born in Germany during World War II. She was the second of five children. Her father was an architect. Her grandfather was a doctor. He taught in medical school. She had a large extended family. Most of them lived nearby. Nusslein-Volhard had a happy childhood. Sometimes her family didn't have extra money to buy fun things. Her parents would make books and toys for the children. She learned to sew her own dresses, too. Her parents were both good musicians. She learned to play the flute.

As a child, Nusslein-Volhard was very interested in plants and animals. She spent a lot of time on a farm. Her grandparents lived there. She would take care of the animals. And she would help with harvesting. At home, she would care for the garden and pets. But she missed having someone explain things to her. So, she tried to find information in books.

Dolly the Sheep

Have you heard of Dolly the sheep? She was the first mammal cloned from an adult cell. She lived for about seven years.

The Electron Microscope

Ernst Ruska was a German physicist. He invented the first electron microscope. He won the Nobel Prize for his invention in 1986.

Electron microscopes help scientists study cells much more closely. They can magnify things up to two million times. They are very expensive to buy and maintain. Even the tiniest speck of dust can interfere with the images created by an electron microscope.

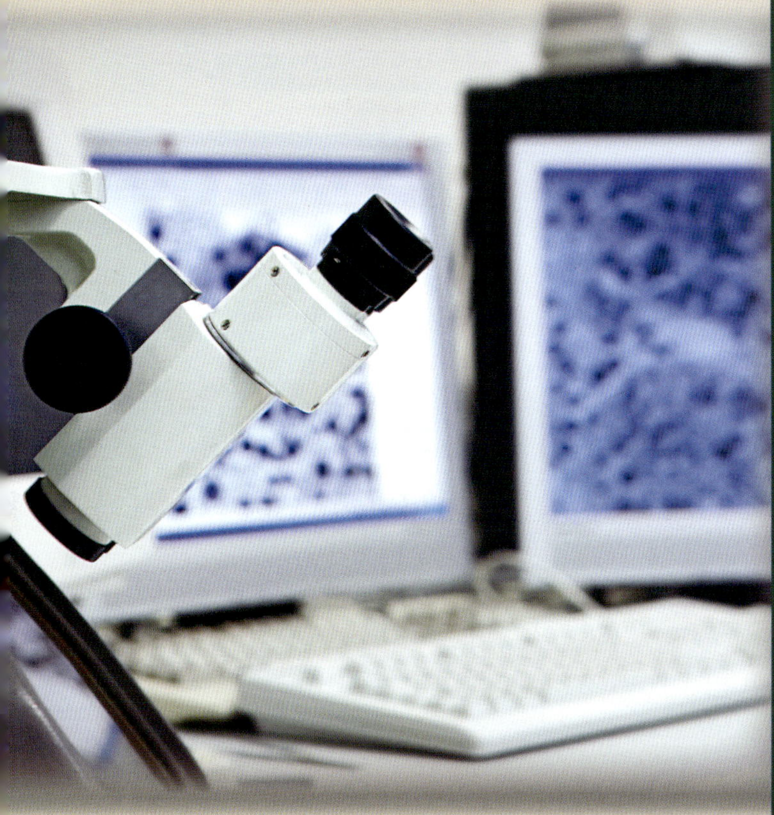

Electron microscopes are widely used in hospitals and laboratories. Many images in this book were taken by an electron microscope.

Nusslein-Volhard loved school. But she was very lazy, and she did little homework. She almost didn't pass her classes! Her teachers knew she was very smart, though. If she was interested in something, she got excellent grades.

After high school, Nusslein-Volhard decided to study **biology**. She wasn't sure if she wanted to be a doctor. So, she took a class at a nursing school. It convinced her not to become a doctor. She took many different science classes. Not all of them interested her. In her last year of school, she took a class on genetics. She thought that was very interesting!

fruit flies

After graduation, she worked in a laboratory and studied DNA and other things, too. Still, she couldn't find something to really grab her interest. She decided to study fruit flies. She wanted to know how a single cell becomes a multicellular organism. She immediately loved working with the flies! She worked with a team to study the flies. The team learned that thousands of genes work together. They control the early development of the fruit fly.

Take a Closer Look

Rosalind Franklin was a British chemist. She used X-rays to study the DNA molecule. She created the first images of DNA. Other scientists used her pictures. They built models of DNA. Thanks to Franklin's pictures, we know how DNA works.

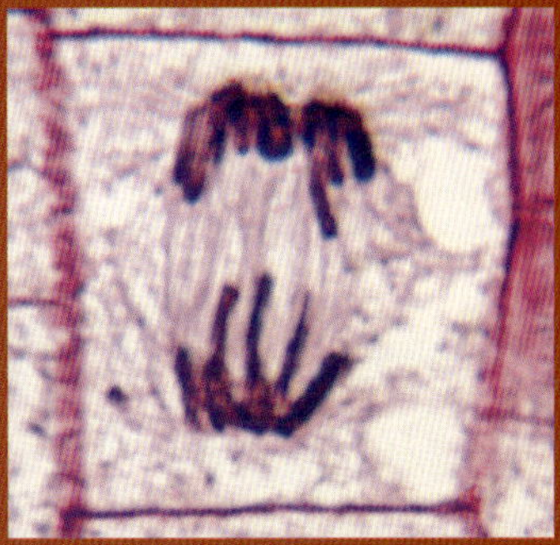

Strange Fact

Cell biology is a strange science. It is the only place where multiplication and division mean the same thing!

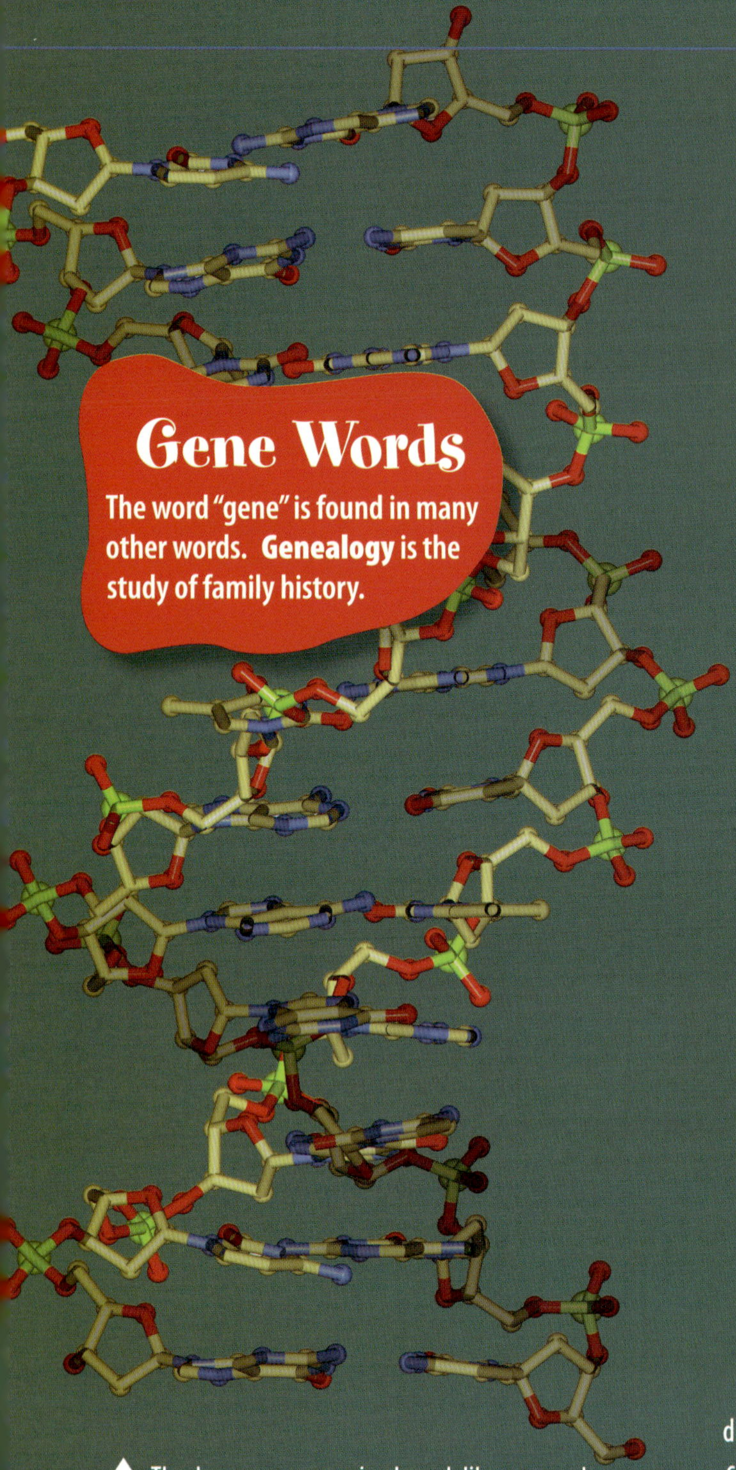

Gene Words

The word "gene" is found in many other words. **Genealogy** is the study of family history.

Nusslein-Volhard and her team started out by damaging genes to cause mutations or birth defects in baby fruit flies. Then they studied what these mutations did to the babies. They bred 40,000 fruit-fly families. They kept thousands of samples of abnormal offspring. They even gave some of them nicknames. Over 20,000 fruit-fly genes were identified. Nearly 5,000 of them are important to early development.

Nusslein-Vohard's work led to new ideas about how the fruit fly develops. Her work is important. It can be applied to all multicellular organisms. It can even apply to humans.

She won the Nobel Prize for her research on genes that cause birth defects.

White blood cells defend the body against diseases like the one attacking this red blood cell. Stem cells can also become white blood cells like the one in the illustration.

The human genome is shaped like a complex spiral ladder. It is called a double helix.

Superman and Stem Cells

Did you know that Superman was a big supporter of stem cell research? Christopher Reeve was an actor. He played Superman in the movies. Then, he had an accident. He was thrown from a horse and paralyzed from the neck down. He was used to flying in the movies. Now, he couldn't even walk. He couldn't move his legs. He worked hard for stem cell research. Many scientists believe that stem cell research can lead to a cure for paralysis and many other problems. Sadly, Reeve died in 2004. He was only 52.

Stem cells renew themselves. They do this through cell division. When stem cells divide, two things can happen. They can remain stem cells. Or, they can become another type of cell. The other cells have specialized jobs. They might be brain cells. Or they could be muscle cells. Scientists want to find ways to use the stem cells to fight diseases and treat injuries.

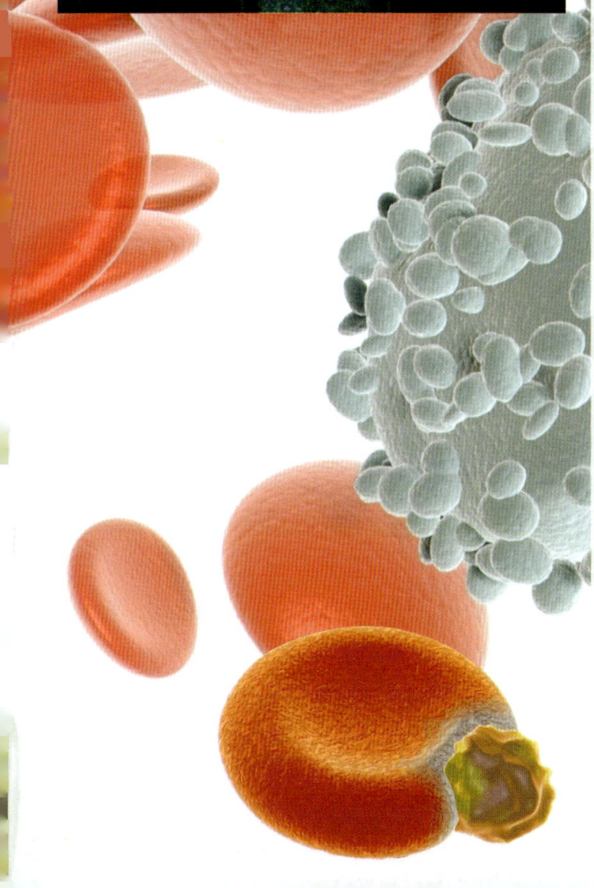

Developmental Biologist: Rita Levi-Montalcini

European Brain Research Institute

Egg-cellent Researcher

When Levi-Montalcini was young, her father expected her to become a wife and mother and stay at home. But at age 20, she decided she wanted to go to medical school. Then, during World War II, Levi-Montalcini was kicked out of her university for being Jewish. So, she set up a small laboratory in her bedroom. She rode her bike to nearby farms to get eggs for her experiments.

Levi-Montalcini is one of seven women who have been awarded the Nobel Prize in medicine.

The bicycling and experimenting paid off. Levi-Montalcini discovered a chemical that tells the nerves in your body where to grow. Her work has helped treat wounds, tumors, and brain diseases. In 1986, she won the Nobel Prize in medicine. She said her success came from doing what she thought was right and being optimistic.

Levi-Montalcini kept tons of eggs in her bedroom.

Being There

Levi-Montalcini made discoveries by studying chicken eggs in her bedroom laboratory. If you could set up a laboratory in your bedroom, what would you study?

Did You Know?

Levi-Montalcini decided to study medicine when her nanny became sick with cancer.

Think About

Levi-Montalcini's discoveries have helped treat many types of injury and disease. What diseases would you like to cure?

Lab: Cell Mobile Models

In this activity, you will make mobile models of plant and animal cells. Common household materials will be used to represent the structures of plant and animal cells. You will identify and describe the structure and function of organelles.

Materials

- construction paper
- crayons or markers
- tape
- wire clothes hangers (2)
- string or yarn
- plastic wrap
- toothpicks
- self-sealing sandwich bag
- notebook paper and pen or pencil

Procedure

1 Make the following animal cell structures: nucleus, smooth ER, rough ER, mitochondria, vacuole, and lysosome. Use construction paper, crayons, and tape if needed to make the cell structures.

2 Attach the cell structures to the clothes hanger, using the string or yarn.

Let's Experiment

3 Wrap the entire model in plastic wrap to represent the cell membrane.

4 Carefully insert toothpicks into the plastic wrap to represent cilia.

5 Attach a long piece of string or yarn to the plastic wrap or clothes hanger to represent a flagellum.

6 Make the following plant cell structures: nucleus, smooth ER, rough ER, mitochondria, chloroplast, vacuole, and lysosome. Use construction paper, crayons, and tape if needed to make the cell structures.

7 Attach the cell structures to the second clothes hanger, using the string or yarn.

8 Wrap the entire model in plastic wrap to represent the cell membrane.

9 Cover the plastic wrap with the self-sealing sandwich bag to represent the cell wall.

10 On a sheet of notebook paper, list all the parts of the cells used in the cell models. Describe the design of your cell parts. The descriptions should explain how your cell parts work together.

Glossary

animalcule—a microscopic organism, such as an amoeba

biology—the scientific study of the natural processes of living things

capillary—a very thin tube, especially one of the smaller tubes that carry blood around the body

cell—the smallest component of life that also lives itself, named after the tiny rooms in monasteries in which monks live

cellula—the tiny rooms in monasteries where monks live

chromosome—a structure made of a coiled DNA molecule, appearing during mitosis and meiosis

DNA—deoxyribonucleic acid; stores the genetic material in a cell's nucleus

gene—a section of DNA that contains the genetic blueprint for a specific trait of an organism

genealogy—the study of the history of the past and present members of a family

genetics—the study of how, in all living things, the characteristics of parents are passed to their children through their genes

meiosis—the process of cell division also called reduction division or sexual reproduction

microbiology—the branch of biology that studies very small living things

mitosis—the process of cell division, or asexual reproduction

monasteries—building in which monks live and worship

nucleus—the organelle containing DNA

organism—a single living thing, such as a plant, animal, or virus

physicist—a person who studies physics (the scientific study of matter and energy)

radiation—a form of energy that comes from a nuclear reaction and can be very dangerous to health

reduction division—the process of cell division, now called meiosis or sexual reproduction

Index

Sally Ride Science

Sally Ride Science™ is an innovative content company dedicated to fueling young people's interests in science. Our publications and programs provide opportunities for students and teachers to explore the captivating world of science—from astrobiology to zoology. We bring science to life and show young people that science is creative, collaborative, fascinating, and fun.

Image Credits

Cover: Bettmann/CORBIS; p.3 Kirsty Pargeter/Shutterstock; p.4 (top) Photos.com; p.4 (left) Bettmann/CORBIS; p.4 sgame/Shutterstock; p.5 (top) Photos.com; p.5 Mary Evans Picture Library/Alamy; p.6 Sebastian Kaulitzki/Shutterstock; pp.6–7 (left) Library of Congress; p.7 (top) The Granger Collection, New York; p.7 (right) Oote Boe Photography/Alamy; p.8 The Print Collector/Alamy; p.9 (left) sgame/Shutterstock; p.9 (right) Photos.com; p.10 SciMAT/Photo Researchers, Inc.; p.11 SuperStock, Inc./SuperStock; p.11 (right) Rick Reason; p.12 (top) Bettmann/CORBIS; p.12 Shutterstock; p.13 Magnus Ehinger/iStockphoto; p.13 (bottom) Rick Reason; p.14 Rodferris/Dreamstime.com; p.15 (left) Tim Bradley; p.15 (top) National Library of Medicine; p.15 (right) Geoff Hardy/Shutterstock; p.16 (top) Sebastian Kaulitzki/Shutterstock; p.16 (left) Ted Spiegel/CORBIS; p.16 (bottom) Arlindo Silva/iStockphoto; p.17 Sebastian Kaulitzki/Shutterstock; p.17 (right) The Granger Collection, New York; pp.18–19 Andrew Paul Leonard/Photo Researchers, Inc.; p.19 Emiliano Rodriguez/Shutterstock; p.20 (top) Franz Pfluegl/Dreamstime.com; p.20 (left) AFP/Getty Images; p.20 (bottom) David C. Rhener/Shutterstock; p.21 (top) Phototake Inc./Alamy; p.21 (bottom) Franz Pfluegl/Dreamstime.com; pp.22–23 Imagemania/Big Stock Photos; p.23 (top) Rick Reason; p.23 (bottom) Photos.com; p.24 Roberto Sanchez/Shutterstock; p.25 (top) Evan Agostini/Getty Images; p.25 Shutterstock; p.26 (top) Nobelstiftelsen; p.26 Photos.com; p.27 Bernard Becker Medical Library; p.28 (top) Sebastian Kaulitzk/Shutterstock; pp.28–29 Nicolle Rager Fuller; p.32 Getty Images